CUBNAPPING
IN KENYA

LOL Detective Club Book #3

By E.M. FINN

CUBNAPPING IN KENYA: LOL DETECTIVE CLUB, BOOK 3

First Edition, June 2016

Cover Illustration by Steven Bybyk and Natalie Khmelvoska
Cover Design by E.M. Finn

Table of Contents

CHAPTER ONE

"I'm so excited to sleep under the stars," Lucy Parker said as she laid her sleeping bag across the wooden floor high up in the trees. Underneath her feet, a giraffe chomped on the leaves that hung below their tree house.

"I just hope a giraffe doesn't lick our feet," Ollie laughed.

"I bet their tongues are like sandpaper. Blech," said Lottie.

The kids were staying in a tree house at the

Safari Wild Animal Park in Kenya, which was a nature preserve on the African plains. Justin Parker, their dad, traveled the world as a photo-journalist and he often took his kids with him on assignment. This time they had travelled to Kenya, a small East African country which is home to animals like elephants, zebras, and lions.

At Safari Park, the animals roamed freely. The best part was that you could sleep in a tree house right alongside them. Safari Park also had a plush hotel for guests who liked hot showers and no chance of giraffes visiting them in the middle of the night.

Their dad had been sent to photograph the newborn Saharan Cheetah cubs who had just been born at the park. The Saharan Cheetah is one of the most endangered animals in the world, with only a few hundred left in the wild.

Mika, the park's resident Saharan Cheetah, had surprised everyone by giving birth to three baby cubs just a few weeks ago.

"I can't believe we get to pet a real cheetah," Lucy said.

Lucy was crazy about animals. She hoped to be a veterinarian when she grew up. That is, if being a detective didn't work out.

Lucy had started the LOL Detective Club with her big brother, Ollie, and her identical twin sister, Lottie. Ollie was ten years old and loved computers. Lucy and Lottie were both eight and a half years old. Lucy was three minutes older than Lottie, which made her the older, wiser sister. Or at least that's what Lucy told Lottie every chance she got.

"When do we get to see Mika and her cubs?" Lottie asked their dad.

"They're introducing the cubs in just a few minutes," Dad said as he gathered up his photography equipment. "There will be quite a few reporters, plus guests from the hotel. Saharan Cheetahs are critically endangered, which means they are very rare."

With their dad, the kids made their way from the tree house over to Cheetah Hill, where Mika lived with her baby cubs. A crowd had already started to gather when a plump man with red cheeks and white hair began speaking over the small crowd that had gathered.

"Hi everybody," he began. "My name is Garth Mabel and I'm the owner of Safari Park. I started this animal preserve twenty years ago. My dream was to build a place where families could come visit animals in a wild habitat. We started with just three animals, and now we've grown to two hundred. Or, two hundred and three if you count Mika's cubs," he smiled.

Ollie hit record on his tablet. "I've got to take a video of this for my blog," he said. "This is the coolest place ever!"

"I can't see," Lottie said as she stood on her tiptoes, trying to look over the heads of all the grown-ups at the front of the crowd.

"Let's stand on this rock," Lucy said.

Ollie, Lottie, and Lucy climbed on top of a huge boulder that overlooked the cheetah's grassy den.

"We have the best view from up here," Lottie said.

Dad looked up at the kids sitting on top of the giant rock.

"Guys, I have to get up in front of the crowd to take photos. I'll see you back at the tree house later this afternoon," he said.

"Okay, dad. Don't get too close to that cheetah. She might eat you," Lottie joked.

Garth kept talking about Safari Park. Ollie wished he'd hurry up so they could see Mika, the cheetah. Just when it looked like Garth was done talking, he turned to a tall lady with leopard print boots.

"Hello, everyone," the woman drawled. "As most of you know, I'm Harley Hanson."

The crowd members began to whisper. Everyone knew that the Hansons had made a lot of money back in the 1800s when they mined for diamonds in South Africa. They had been living off their riches ever since. Harley Hanson was known for partying and made frequent appearances in the gossip newspapers.

"My grandfather loved animals. That's why he decided to donate so much money to keep Safari Park's doors open. Without my grandfather, Safari Park would've been doomed years ago," Harley said as Garth coughed quickly.

"Thank you so much, Ms. Hanson," Garth said as he cleared his throat. The two people standing next to Garth started to fidget nervously. They were both wearing official Safari Park uniforms.

"Who are they?" Lucy whispered.

"Oh, I saw them earlier on the Safari Park website," Lottie said. "The short guy with blue hair is Artie Mack. He takes care of the ani-

put her to sleep, I bet."

Within seconds, Mika was fast asleep in a patch of warm sun. Dr. Long held Mika's head and patted her behind her ears. She whispered something to Mika, but the kids couldn't hear what she said.

"Well, folks, that was exciting! It's okay, everything is under control," Garth said nervously to the scattered crowd. "She'll be sleeping for a little while, so why don't you all go back to the hotel and grab a bite to eat at the restaurant? We've got a nice special today."

Garth let out a long sigh, and the crowd started to leave. Artie walked back to Mika's den where she had been napping with her cubs earlier. A second later, he ran out of the tall grass yelling and waving his arms.

"Mika's babies are gone! All three cubs have been kidnapped," Artie screamed.

Garth's eyes got huge and his skin turned bright red.

"There must be some mistake," he gasped.

"Look, whoever did it left a ransom note," Artie said as he handed Garth a thin piece of paper. Garth stared at the paper in shock.

"They've been Cub-napped!" Lottie shouted.

CHAPTER TWO

"Who would do such a thing?" Lucy whimpered. "They're just innocent little cubs. You heard what Dr. Long said. They need their mama."

Garth turned to the crowd, who had returned to the hill after hearing Artie's screams.

"Everyone, I'm afraid the meet and greet with Mika's cubs is cancelled for now. Please go back to your rooms at Safari Hotel or to your tree houses. We'll let you know when we have more information."

As soon as the crowd cleared, Garth, Dr. Long, Harley Hanson, and Artie huddled together on the grassy plain. Harley Hanson dabbed her eyes as she looked out across the sweeping landscape.

"Whoever could have done this? My grand-daddy would be so upset," Harley sobbed.

Lottie, Ollie, and Lucy climbed down off the huge stone boulder where they'd been sitting.

"Well, that's rotten," Ollie said.

"What's going to happen to those babies without their mama's milk?" Lucy worried. "I hope they're going to be okay."

"I don't know," Lottie sighed. "It's bad enough that they're babies. But, Saharan chee-tahs are almost extinct."

"I'm going to write a story for my blog," Ollie said. "Maybe one of my readers will help us solve this case."

"You'll help me solve the mystery?" Lucy's eyes lit up. Lucy loved solving mysteries more than anything else in the world.

"Of course, I will. I want Mika's babies back home with their mama," he said quietly.

"Let's talk to Garth and see what he says," Lottie said. "Maybe he can give us some clues."

Garth was standing against a tree, wiping his forehead with a handkerchief.

"Excuse me, Mr. Mabel," Lucy said. "I know this may be a bad time, but we were hoping we could help find Mika's cubs."

"Oh, you guys are sweet. I'm afraid it's just a terrible situation," he said.

"Well, hopefully the police can help," Ollie said. "Has anybody called them yet?"

Garth looked worried. "No, I haven't called the police. And I'm not going to."

He handed the ransom note to Ollie, who read the neatly typed words:

You will get Mika's cubs back when you transfer

six million dollars to an offshore bank account in
the Caribbean. No funny business. Don't go to the
police or you'll never see the cubs again. You have
until sundown.

"Six million dollars?" Lucy gasped. "That's a
lot of money."

"You bet it is," Garth said. "It's all the money Harley Hanson's grandad left to Safari Park.
Without his donation, I'll have to close my
doors. We were broke until he gave us money."

"What will happen to the animals?" Lottie
said.

"We'll have to sell them to cover our losses,"
Garth sighed. "Then, I'll have to sell Safari
Park."

"No more animals?" Lucy said with tears
welling in her eyes.

"I'm afraid not," he said.

"Why can't you talk to the police?" Lottie
asked.

Ollie rubbed his eyebrow. "Probably because

the thief doesn't want to get caught, that's why."

"That's exactly right, Ollie. The kidnapper clearly knows Saharan Cheetah cubs are rare and priceless. Whoever it is could sell them to animal collectors. I bet they could get two million dollars apiece for each cub," Garth said.

"Wow," the kids all said at the same time. "Those are expensive cheetahs!"

"The kidnapper wants us to send the money to a bank account in the Caribbean so it can't be traced," Garth said.

"Yea, I guess six million dollars is too much money to put in a briefcase," Lucy said.

"I'll say," Garth sighed. He looked into the sky at the sun high on the horizon. "It's nearly noon right now, and the sun will be down in about nine hours."

"Good thing the sun stays up longer in the summer," Ollie said.

"Yea, good thing. Still, that's not a lot of

time," Lucy whispered.

Garth scratched his head as he frowned.

"I guess I'd better go figure out what to do. Seems like I don't have much choice. Safari Park has been a dream of mine for so long. I'll be sad to shut the doors," Garth said as his voice trailed off.

Ollie leaned against the fence next to Mika's cage.

"I'm really sorry," he said. "We're going to do our best to help find the kidnapper."

As Ollie looked down at his shoe, something shiny glinted in the sunlight. He kicked the shiny thing underneath the tall grass, but instead of flying, it stuck to his hiking boot.

"Ollie, look at your foot," Lucy gasped.

A long needle, the kind a doctor uses for shots, stuck straight out from the sole of Ollie's brown boot.

"What in the world?" Garth said. "What's a needle doing here?"

"I think it's a clue," Lucy said. "Who knows, there may be more clues hiding here. Do you mind if we take a look around?"

"Sure, no problem. Just make sure to keep your distance from Mika. We don't know when she'll wake up," Garth said.

Mika snoozed peacefully in the sunlit grass, her paw covering her head.

"She was one mad mama," Ollie said.

"It's okay, Mika. We're going to find your babies really soon," Lucy said.

"What, do you speak cheetah now, Lucy?" Ollie laughed.

"I'm trying to," Lucy giggled.

The kids bent down and cleared a path around Ollie's boot. There was a lot of dirt and dead grass where the needle was found. They searched for a while longer, and almost gave up, when Lottie suddenly found a piece of clear rubber.

"Guys, I think you should see this," Lottie

said.

"What is it?" asked Lucy.

"I don't know," Lottie said. "But it's the only plastic around here. It looks like it could be a clue."

"I know what that is," Ollie exclaimed. "I remember it from when you guys were babies. That's the top to a baby bottle. Dad used to feed you bottles all the time." He turned the plastic over in his fingers. "Or at least, part of the top to a baby bottle. It looks like it got ripped."

Lucy pointed up to the top of a nearby tree.

"It looks like the other part is up there," she said as she pointed to some clear plastic hanging from a branch."

"You would never see it if you weren't hunting for it," Lottie said.

"Looks like another clue," Lucy said. "I bet whoever stole the cubs is feeding them with baby bottles since they're too young to eat regular food."

"How would the kidnapper get cheetah milk into a bottle?" Lottie wondered.

"Maybe they're using regular milk or baby formula to feed the cubs until they get the ransom money. Do you remember that one time we found some lost kittens?" Ollie asked.

"Oh, right! The veterinarian told us to bottle feed them until we found their mama. I guess cheetahs are like big cats, so maybe that would work, too," Lucy said.

"Yeah maybe," Ollie said as he scratched his forehead. "I wish you really could speak cheetah, Lucy. Then Mika could tell us who kidnapped the baby cubs."

"Don't worry, Mika. We'll figure out who the cub-napper is," Lucy purred to the sleeping cheetah.

"Cub-napper?" Ollie laughed.

"What? It makes sense. A kid is a human," Lucy said.

"Or a goat. Baby goats are kids," Lottie said.

Lottie knew a lot about baby animals since she'd read every book she could find about them.

"Right. Baby cheetahs are called cubs. So I'm calling this a cub-napping," Lucy smiled.

"I have the strangest sister in the world," Ollie laughed as he patted Lucy on the back.

CHAPTER THREE

"All this detective work is making me hungry," Lottie said as her stomach gurgled. "Let's go back to the hotel and have lunch."

Safari Park had a restaurant right in the center of the hotel. The main dining room had fancy tables with waiters and white table cloths. Around back was an open air snack shack where you could grab burgers and fries.

"Fancy hotel or snack shack?" Ollie asked.

"What do you think?" Lottie giggled.

"Burgers and fries sound good to me," he said, and he led them around to the back of the hotel.

"I'll have a cheeseburger with no meat. I'm a vegetarian," Lucy said when she ordered at the counter.

"You want a what?" sputtered the man behind the counter. "How about a grilled cheese?"

"Sure, that works," Lucy smiled.

Ollie, Lottie, and Lucy crowded around a picnic table as they ate their fries and grilled cheese sandwiches.

"Where do you think we'll find the kidnapper? We don't have much time," Ollie said as he chewed with his mouth open.

"Gross, Ollie!" Lucy said as she scrunched up her nose.

"The cubs must be around here somewhere," Lottie said. She looked under the picnic table, as if one of the cubs had crawled underneath it.

"I don't think they're under the table," Ollie

laughed. "The cubs could have been stolen by anyone. Six million dollars is a lot of money."

"It sure is," Lucy said. "We need to figure out who stole Mika's cubs."

"And what that doctor's needle had to do with the kidnapping," Ollie said. "I wonder if the kidnapper used the needle to make Mika fall asleep when he stole the cubs."

"He or *she* stole the cubs," Lottie corrected him. "It could have been a guy or a girl."

"That's true," Ollie said. "Whoever did it had access to a needle and the medicine to make Mika fall asleep. I mean, that's not the kind of thing you find at a store."

"We should ask Dr. Long if she's missing any supplies from her medical bag," Lucy said. "Unless, of course, she's the kidnapper. Then, why would she tell us the truth?"

"But why would Dr. Long steal the cubs? She loves animals," Lottie said.

"Maybe she'd love six million dollars more,"

Ollie chuckled.

"Let's add her to our list of suspects. We'll interview her later and see if her story checks out," Lucy said.

"Have you guys thought that maybe it was somebody from outside Safari Park who stole the cubs? They could have snuck in at night when everyone was sleeping," Lucy said.

"Impossible. I read on the website that Safari Park is surrounded by electronic fences. Nobody can get in or out except through the main gate. So, it has to be an inside job," Lottie said.

"Maybe it's a guest at the hotel," Ollie said. "Who wouldn't want to take a cheetah cub home as a pet? Until it's full-grown, anyway."

"The kidnapper could be a guest," Lucy said. "We could pretend to be maids and search everybody's room back at the Safari hotel."

"That will take hours," Ollie said. "We don't have time for that. There's got to be a quicker way to find the cubs. We only have until sundown, remember?"

The kids munched their fries in silence as they thought. Then, Ollie turned on his tablet and said, "Let's watch the video I took this morning of Mika. Maybe we can see if she's drugged or not. Or maybe there's a suspicious person in the crowd that we didn't notice before."

Lottie reached into Ollie's fries and grabbed a handful.

"Hey, those are mine," Ollie said as Lottie slid a few fries onto her plate.

Lottie smiled at him. "Please?" she asked sweetly.

"Oh, alright," he huffed.

The kids watched as Garth gave his speech on the video. Next to him on Cheetah Hill stood Dr. Long, Harley Hanson, and Artie. Garth's plump red cheeks puffed out as he spoke.

"Skip past this part," Lucy said impatiently. "I want to see the part where Mika jumps at the crowd."

Ollie inched the video forward to Mika's green eyes peering out of the den. She sniffed the air, and then her eyes looked straight ahead.

"Mika's looking straight at Dr. Long," Lottie shouted. "I knew it was the veterinarian who stole the cubs."

"Lottie, Dr. Long is standing right next to Garth, Harley Hanson, and Artie. It could be any one of them," Ollie sighed.

"True, it could be. But look, Mika's not paying any attention to the rest of the crowd. She looks like she wants to kill Dr. Long. This is a great place for us to start," Lottie said.

"It looks like the LOL Detective Club is one step closer to solving our mystery," Lucy smiled.

CHAPTER FOUR

"This makes no sense," Lottie huffed. "Why would Dr. Long want to steal the cubs?"

I can think of six million reasons why," Ollie said.

"We don't know for sure it was Dr. Long. It could have just as easily been Artie or Harley Hanson. They were all bunched together on Cheetah Hill. Mika could have been staring at any one of them."

Lucy munched on a French fry while she

frowned.

"Poor Mika. She looked so upset," Lucy said. "I don't blame her for wanting to attack."

"But how could one of those people have stolen the cubs when they were standing up on Cheetah Hill the whole time?" Lottie said.

"They probably stole the cubs earlier in the day, hid the cubs, and then acted surprised when they were kidnapped," Lucy said.

"I bet Mika saw the kidnapper and recognized him," Ollie said.

"Or maybe Mika smelled the kidnapper," Lottie said as she scrunched up her nose.

"Smelled him?" Ollie scratched his head.

"Saharan cheetahs have an excellent sense of smell," Lottie read from a website on Ollie's tablet. "They can catch their prey even when they're blindfolded."

"Who would blindfold a cheetah?" Ollie laughed.

Lucy looked at Ollie sideways. "What else

does it say?" Lucy asked.

"Cheetah cubs nurse for four months. After that, they start eating meat," Lottie read.

"Mika's cubs are only three weeks old. No wonder the cub-napper brought baby bottles," Lucy said. "Sounds like whoever stole the cubs knew what he was doing."

"He or *she* was doing," Lottie said.

"Right," Ollie smiled.

"Well, Artie knows all about feeding the cubs. He would know how to bottle feed them better than anyone," Lucy said.

"And he could have stolen the needle from Dr. Long' bag," Lottie said.

"He could have. Artie is always around when Dr. Long checks in on the cubs. Remember, Garth told us that," Ollie said.

"That's right, he did," Lucy remembered. "The first thing we should do is talk to Artie. Even if he didn't do it, he might help us figure out who did."

"But won't he suspect us if we start snooping around asking questions? That would make him clam up instantly," Lucy said.

"Not if we tell him I'm interviewing him for my blog," Ollie smiled.

"Excellent," Lucy shouted.

Ollie put his hand in the French fry basket but it was empty.

"Lottie, did you eat my very last French fry?" he huffed.

"Yup, you caught me," Lottie smiled.

"Well, that's one mystery we've solved for the day," Lucy giggled.

The kids cleaned up the lunch mess and headed over to Artie's office.

On the way, they passed giraffes, rhinos, and a huge elephant with long white tusks.

"Do you think the cheetah cubs could have run away?" Ollie asked.

"Not a chance. They're barely walking," Lottie said. "Besides, I read that cheetah cubs don't leave the den until they're at least two months old."

"And don't forget about the ransom note," Lucy said. "I know cheetahs are smart, but I don't think they can write ransom notes asking for six million dollars."

The kids found Artie shoveling elephant poop behind one of the big barns on the property. He was knee deep in elephant poop and the whole place stunk.

"Hi Artie," Lucy said as she tried not to gag.

Her eyes watered from the stench but she tried not to show it.

"Is this a bad time? Ollie is writing a blog post and we'd love to ask you a few questions," Lottie said as she finished her sister's sentence.

"Oh, sure, no problem," Artie said. "I'm just sending off the elephant dung to be recycled."

"Recycled?" Lucy gasped.

"Oh yes, a farm down the way takes elephant poop and makes it into paper," Artie laughed.

"Oh my gross," Lottie said. "People write on poop?"

"About anything you can think of can be recycled," Artie said. "I just wish it wasn't so smelly."

"I'll say," Lucy said as she tried not to barf.

"We were wondering if you knew anything about the cub-napping, I mean kidnapping, of the Saharan cheetah cubs," Lucy said.

Artie started to fidget and his brow turned wet with sweat. Or maybe it was just the smell of elephant poop that made him look sick.

"What do you want to know about it?" he said.

Lottie, Ollie, and Lucy looked at each other nervously.

"Well, I'm writing about it on my blog and I wanted to see if you saw anything strange or heard anything unusual," Ollie said.

"Nothing unusual at all. I put out Mika's

food and water last night. When I checked on Mika this morning, all the cubs were sleeping on her. Then, I went to check on the other animals. After that, I met up with everyone on Cheetah Hill to introduce the cubs," Artie said.

"Do you think the cubs will be alright?" Lucy asked as her lip quivered.

"Well, it depends. If the kidnapper can feed them, they'll do fine," Artie said.

"And how would the kidnapper feed them?" Ollie asked, fingering the plastic baby bottle top he had stuffed into his back pocket.

"Oh, I don't know. Probably feed them from a baby bottle. I had to do that for our giraffe, Mille, when her mama died," he said quietly.

"That's awful," Lucy said as she frowned. "Did you see anyone going into Mika's den?"

"Well, that's just it. I didn't see anybody. Dr. Long was with Mika yesterday giving her a regular checkup. But other than that, nobody's been to Mika's den at all."

Ollie jotted down a few notes on his tablet.

"I sure hope they find Mika's cubs," Artie sighed. "I can't imagine who would do something so awful."

"Me, too," Lucy said slowly.

"Listen guys, I've got to get back to my um…elephant dung," Artie said as he wrinkled his nose. "With the hot African sun blazing, it only gets smellier by the minute."

"Okay, well, thanks for helping us," Ollie said as he went to shake Artie's hand.

"Um, I don't think you want to do that," Artie said. "Unless you want some elephant poop on your hand."

"Thanks but no thanks," Ollie laughed.

The kids walked down the path away from Artie and the elephant poop.

"The coast is clear," Ollie whispered as soon as they were out of earshot.

"So, do you think Artie did it?" Lucy whispered.

"I don't think so. But, he sure could use the money. Shoveling elephant poop is not what I'd call a fun job," Ollie said.

"Let's go talk to Dr. Long," Lottie said. "She's the one with the needles. Besides, if anyone knows about feeding baby animals, I'll be she does."

"It's got to be her," Ollie said.

"Right. She was with the cubs this morning. She has the medicine to make Mika drowsy."

"We should have the police arrest her right now," Lottie said.

"What, and risk hurting the cubs? Don't you remember what the ransom note said?" Lucy frowned.

"We have to get Dr. Long to tell us where she's hidden the cubs. Then, we can rescue them," Lottie said.

"Or we could just lock Dr. Long up and throw away the key," Lucy huffed. "Then she couldn't hurt the cubs."

"I know you're mad. But listen, you've got to think with a clear head if we're going to save those baby cubs," Ollie said. "Just act cool when you see Dr. Long, okay?"

The kids strode up to the Animal Hospital at the edge of Safari Park.

"Hey kids," Dr. Long said. "Have you come to check out the Animal Hospital? This is where we take care of all the sick animals."

"Do you have a lot of sick animals here?" Lucy asked, trying to sound casual.

"Well, not a lot. But, everybody gets sick sometimes. I can give you a tour of the hospital, if you'd like."

"Sure, we'd love it," Ollie said as he whipped out his tablet.

Dr. Long walked through the hospital, showing the kids the stalls for the sick animals.

"We keep the smaller animals in here when they're sick," Dr. Long said. "The bigger animals can't fit. I once tried to stuff a rhino into a hospital bed, but that didn't work out too well," she laughed.

"Artie told us you saw Mika this morning," Ollie said. "Did she look sick to you?"

Dr. Long bit her lip. "Well, I was going to check on her this morning before everyone showed up. But, she was sleeping and I didn't want to disturb her. Sleeping is normal for a mother who's just given birth."

"We were thinking she might have been drugged," Lottie said.

"Drugged?" Dr. Long frowned. "Why would someone do that?"

"We were hoping you could tell us," Lucy said. "We found a medical needle in the grass by her den."

"Oh my," Dr. Long said as her eyes grew wide. "Let me check my medicine cabinet and see if anything has been stolen."

Dr. Long fished her keys out of her pocket. "Looks like everything is here," she said as she checked the shelves of her medicine cabinet.

"Is there anybody you can think of who would want to steal the cubs?" Ollie asked.

"Sometimes we get locals who break into Safari Park," Dr. Long said. "But I talked to Garth and he said there were no break-ins last night.'

"Maybe someone snuck into the park and Garth didn't realize it," Ollie said.

"I don't think so," Dr. Long said. "If you don't know where Mika's den is, you wouldn't be able to find it. It's pretty well-hidden. We planned it that way to give her some privacy."

"Thanks for talking to us," Lottie said. "I'm glad to know that your medicine wasn't stolen." As Lottie turned to leave, she saw an empty bottle of medicine in the trash.

"What's that?" Lottie said as she pointed to the bottle.

"Err, that's nothing," Dr. Long stammered. "I had a lion who injured his paw a few days ago, and I had to give him stitches. That medicine knocked him out so I could stitch him up," she said.

She tossed a napkin into the garbage can so it covered up the empty bottle.

"I've been meaning to take out the recycling."

An awkward silence hung in the air, as the kids eyed the garbage can.

"I'm going to go check Mika out right now. I want to see if she's really been drugged. I'll be able to tell by the pupils of her eyes," Dr. Long announced.

"Can we come with you?" Ollie asked.

"I don't see why not," Dr. Long said. "But, you'd better stay back when we get close. Mika's still pretty angry that her cubs are missing."

"Great! I can't wait to see Mika and tell her we're on the case," Lucy smiled.

Dr. Long furrowed her eyebrow. "On second thought, I don't want you guys to get hurt.

Maybe it would be better for everybody if you stayed away until we find the cubs."

Ollie, Lucy, and Lottie walked out of the Animal Hospital no closer to finding the cubs than they'd been when they arrived.

As the door closed behind them, Ollie said, "Well, that was weird. Did you see how nervous she got when you pointed out that medicine in the trash?"

"Did I ever," Lucy said. "Dr. Long is acting completely guilty."

"And then she wouldn't let us go see Mika. There's something fishy going on with her," Lottie sighed.

CHAPTER FIVE

"What do you say we follow Dr. Long? We can see if she's really going to check in on Mika," Ollie said.

"That sounds like a great idea, Ollie," Lucy and Lottie whispered at the same time.

They waited in the bushes behind the Animal Hospital for Dr. Long to come outside.

Just then, they overheard a shrill voice coming from around the corner.

"Finally! I've been trying to call you for an

hour. My phone barely gets any service out here," the woman huffed. "I can't wait to get back to civilization. All this dust is ruining my complexion."

Ollie peeked out from behind the bushes, making sure he wasn't seen.

"It's Harley Hanson, the heiress whose grandfather donated the money to Safari Park," Ollie said.

"Sounds like she's is not a happy camper," Lottie laughed.

"The money is coming in tonight, don't you worry about that," Harley whispered. "And if we don't get the money, we can make the cubs into a nice, fur coat."

Ollie, Lottie, and Lucy's eyes got big.

"Listen darling, I have to go. This humidity is frizzing my hair. I'm going to get a cocktail in the lounge and rest by a fan. Kisses," Harley cooed into the phone.

She slapped some mosquitos as she hung up

and headed back to the fancy restaurant.

"Did you hear that?" Lucy whispered. "She admitted to stealing the cubs."

"Except it's our word against hers. Did you happen to get her confession on video?" Lottie asked.

Ollie shook his head no. "I sure wish I had."

Lucy clapped her hands together.

"Change of plans. Instead of following Dr. Long to see Mika, it's Operation Confession time," Lucy said.

"Operation what?" Ollie asked.

"We've got to get her to admit on video that she stole those cubs," Lucy explained.

Ollie frowned. "She'll never do that. But maybe if we interview her, we can figure out where she hid the cubs. That's all the proof we need."

"Great idea, Ollie. It looks like she's headed to the dining room. Let's follow her," Lottie whispered.

Ollie, Lottie, and Lucy crept out of the bushes behind the Animal Hospital and followed closely behind Harley Hanson.

She slid into a booth at the restaurant and ordered a tall fruity drink. She was looking at her phone when Ollie, Lottie, and Lucy sat down at the table next to her.

Ollie dropped his napkin on the floor and turned around.

"Oh my goodness," he exclaimed. "Are you Harley Hanson? The famous Harley Hanson?"

The woman blushed. "Why, yes, I am. I didn't think anyone would recognize me here."

"Well, I'm such a fan," Ollie gushed. "I'm Ollie Parker and these are my twin sisters, Lottie and Lucy."

"Pleasure to meet you," Harley said. "Are you kids enjoying your stay at Safari Park?"

Lottie and Lucy looked annoyed at Ollie, who continued making small talk with Harley Hanson.

"Ollie, aren't we supposed to be..." Lucy whispered.

"You'll have to excuse my sister," Ollie said. "I have a blog, and it would be a dream of mine to interview you. If you have the time, of course," he said.

"Anything for one of my fans," she smiled. Ollie slid into the booth next to her.

"So, how long are you staying at Safari Park?" Ollie smiled.

"Just until tomorrow," Zoe said. "I have got to get out of this heat. I only came to see the cheetah cubs."

Ollie took down notes on his tablet.

"What are you writing?" she said suspiciously.

"Oh, I'm just taking notes for my blog article. It's all about the missing cheetahs," Ollie said. "You wouldn't know anything about that, would you?" he gulped.

"My goodness, no!" Harley said, looking as

if she might faint. "Imagine someone taking those babies from their mother. It's awful."

As they spoke, Lottie crawled under the table and began to peek through Harley's purse. Inside, she saw an opened packet of baby formula and an empty bottle of sleeping pills. Lottie stuffed them into her pocket. They made a crinkling noise as she scooted back out from under the table.

"What was that?" Harley said suddenly.

"Oh, I was just, um, fidgeting with my, um, tablet," Ollie said. "It makes noises like that sometimes. As I was saying…" Ollie gulped.

Lottie slid her stomach onto the floor. When she was almost out from under the table, her arm accidentally brushed Harley's ankle.

The hairs on Harley's neck stood on end.

"Did you feel that?" she said as her eyes froze.

"What?" Ollie said. "No, I didn't feel anything."

"It felt like a cat was brushing across my leg," Harley said as she swatted at her leg.

Lottie crawled out from under the table and inched back into her chair.

"Must be the air conditioning in here," Ollie said nervously.

Lottie sat at the table with Lucy, barely able to hold in her giggles. Just then, Harley's phone rang.

"I really must take this call," she said. "If you'll excuse me."

"Oh, of course," Ollie said. "We have to get back to our tree house anyway."

The kids left the restaurant in silence. The second they closed the door and were safely outside, Lucy and Lottie started screaming.

"Look what I found in her bag," Lottie gasped. "Baby formula and sleeping pills. She's got to be the one who kidnapped Mika's cubs."

"We should go to the police," Ollie said. "We have all the evidence we need."

"I agree. But listen, we still don't know where MIka's cubs are hidden. What if she hurts them? You heard what she said about making them into a fur coat," Lucy said.

The kids were quiet for a minute as they thought about what to do next.

"The cubs have to be close. Where do you think she'd hide them?" Ollie asked.

"Well, she couldn't have hidden them in her room because the maids would've found them by now," Lucy said.

Lottie's stomach rumbled. "I'm getting hungry again. When can we eat next?"

"I bet those cubs are hungry, too. They're probably meowing up a storm. Hungry kittens are loud, and I bet that hungry cheetahs are even louder." Lucy frowned.

"Right. So, where would you hide them, if you were her?" Ollie asked.

"Safari Park is huge. The cubs could be anywhere," Lottie said.

"Maybe we should follow Harley around, and see if she goes to feed them. I bet she'll be checking in on them before too long," said Ollie.

"How can we follow her without looking too suspicious?" Lucy said.

"We could wear disguises," Lottie squealed.

"Somehow, I think she'd figure that out," Lucy giggled.

Ollie scratched his head as he thought for a minute. "I bet there's a clue on her phone that will lead us to the cubs."

"You want to steal Harley Hanson's cell phone?" Lottie gulped.

"Borrow her phone, not steal it," Ollie said. "We'll give it back after we've found the cubs."

"Or we'll give it to the police," Lucy said.

"But, how are we going to take Harley's phone without her knowing?" Lottie asked.

"I've got the perfect plan," Ollie smiled.

CHAPTER SIX

Just then, Harley Hanson walked by the front desk. Her high heels clicked on the cool marble tiles of the hotel lobby floor.

"I'm going to the spa," she said to the hotel clerk. "I'll have the mud mask facial. Make sure Max keeps the mud warm this time," she huffed.

As Harley as she walked down the hall towards the spa, the kids tiptoed behind her and hid in open doorways. After a short walk,

Harley turned into a dimly lit room that smelled of lavender and had a massage table in the middle of it.

Lottie, Ollie and Lucy peeked through the barely open door and watched Harley go into the bathroom. Moments later, Harley came out in a white robe, with her leopard print purse slung over her shoulder.

"I wonder if her purse is made of real leopard fur?" Lottie whispered.

Harley flung her purse under the massage table. It fell half open and Harley's phone peeked out of the top.

"Ollie, grab her phone before she sees us," Lucy said. Quietly, Ollie opened the door and crept into the room. He tiptoed towards the purse.

Suddenly a tall man walked around a corner and headed directly towards Lucy and Lottie.

"Someone's coming!" Lucy whispered. The two girls quickly stepped away from the door and acted innocent. The man walked straight past them and into the spa room. Ollie dove under the massage table just in time for the man not to notice him.

"That was close," Lottie whispered.

Ollie tried to make himself as small as possible under the table. He wrapped his arms around his knees and curled tightly into a ball. He didn't notice his tablet falling out of his back pocket and right into Harley's wide open purse.

"Will you be having the usual today, Miss Hanson?" the man asked.

"Oh yes, Max. I need a mud mask like you wouldn't believe," she said. "And make sure it's warm mud this time. Last time it was freezing cold, and that does nothing for my skin."

Max rolled his eyes when Harley wasn't looking.

"Sure thing, Miss Hanson," he said quietly. He smeared some warm mud across Harley's face and placed cucumbers over her closed eyes. "I'll be back in a few minutes to check on you," he said, and walked out the door.

Harley relaxed on top of the massage table, still unaware of Ollie. She hummed a tune to herself as she waited for Max to return.

Just as Ollie reached inside Harley's purse, her phone started beeping loudly.

"I forgot to turn off my phone," Harley sighed.

With the cucumbers still over her eyes, Harley reached inside her purse as Ollie quickly scooted out of the way. She turned off her phone and rolled back up to the top of the massage table.

Ollie's forehead beaded with sweat. He looked like he was about to throw up.

"That was too close," he mouthed, as Lottie and Lucy peered through the crack in the doorway.

"Throw me her phone," Lucy whispered.

"We need proof she stole the cubs!"

Ollie grabbed Harley's phone out of her purse and tossed it to Lucy, but his aim was off. The phone knocked into a table lamp, which flew down onto the floor with a crash.

"What was that?" Harley jumped. "Is everything okay?" She still had cucumbers over her eyes, and she couldn't see a thing. In the confusion, Lucy snatched up the phone.

"Ahem, yes, Miss Hanson," Ollie said in a low voice. He was pretending to be Max, but his voice quivered as he spoke. "Just relax and get some rest."

"My mud mask is getting cold. I need a refresh," Harley said impatiently.

Ollie looked at Lucy and Lottie. "What do I do?" he mouthed as he shook his head.

"Put some mud on her face," Lucy mouthed back.

Ollie tiptoed over to an open window and looked down at a big pile of mud warming in the sun. He reached out, scooped up a wet handful, and brought it back inside the room. He sniffed it and made a face. It was elephant dung.

"Ewww," Ollie wretched at the stinky pile of poop. With his free hand, he grabbed a bottle and spritzed a few squirts of lavender perfume on it to make it smell better.

"Here we go," Ollie whispered as he smeared the elephant poop across Harley's face.

"Max, this is marvelous," Harley gasped as Ollie spread warm elephant poop across her cheeks.

Meanwhile, Lucy turned on Harley's phone and began snooping. In the pictures folder, she found photos of the three cheetah cubs rolled up in white blankets.

Just then, Lottie and Lucy heard the sound of footsteps approaching. It was Max on his way back with fresh mud for Harley's mud mask.

"Uh-oh," Lucy mouthed. "Ollie, get out of there!"

"Where should I go?" Ollie said as he danced around the room.

"Follow me," Lottie mouthed. She quietly crept into the room, dragging Lucy with her. She pointed at the closet on the other side of the room. All three kids tiptoed into the closet, just as Max entered the room with the warm mask.

"What is that awful smell?" Max said as he held his nose. He looked over at the pile of mud on Harley Hanson's face and his eyes got wide.

"Oh my," he said.

Harley bolted straight up on the massage table and threw the cucumbers off her eyes.

"What's going on here?" she shouted. "I'm trying to relax and I keep getting disturbed. I could have you fired!"

"I'm so sorry," Max said. His lip trembled. "How do you, um, like your mud mask?" he asked nervously.

"It's the best I've ever had," she smiled.

Lucy, Ollie, and Lottie peeked out from a crack in the closet door. They couldn't help but giggle when they realized Ollie really had put elephant poop on Harley's face.

All of a sudden, Lottie let out a loud snort. Lucy threw her hands over Lottie's mouth, but it was too late. Harley had heard her.

"What was that?" Harley said.

"I don't know," Max said. "It could be one of the animals. It sounded like a rhinoceros."

Ollie quietly shut the closet door and whispered to his sisters.

"That was close. Lucy, see what else you can find on Harley's phone. Once Harley is done with her massage, we'll sneak out of the closet and take the evidence to Garth."

"Great idea," Lottie said. "Hopefully, this mud mask will be over soon."

Lucy jiggled the door handle.

"Guys, it looks like we might have a bigger problem than we thought," she gulped.

"What is it now?" Ollie said.

Tears started to well up in Lucy's eyes.

"We're locked inside the closet. We'll never be able to get out in time to save the cubs."

CHAPTER SEVEN

"What do you mean, we're locked inside the closet?" Ollie said as he jiggled the door handle.

Ollie tried turning the handle a few times. It wouldn't budge.

"Oh, now I see what you mean," he said slowly.

The storage closet where the kids were hiding was tall with a small light at the very top. There were no windows or vents. Fresh towels were stacked in the corner, along with a few plates of green cucumbers.

"Well, at least we have snacks," Lottie said pointing to the cucumbers.

"Lottie, those are for putting on your eyes when you have a mud mask. They're not for eating," Lucy said.

"Right," Lottie mumbled as she munched the end of a cucumber.

"How are we going to get out of here?" Lucy sighed. "There's no way out. Unless we knock down the door."

"But then Harley will see us and we'll be in a lot of trouble for stealing her phone," Ollie said.

Through the door they heard soft music playing while Harley enjoyed her spa treatment.

"Guys, we have to be quiet or else Harley will discover us hiding in here," Lucy said.

The kids sat in silence as they thought of what to do next. The closet was very cramped, and it was hard to stay so quiet.

"I know what to do. We can call Garth on

Harley's phone and tell him she's the kidnapper," Lottie said.

"Great idea," Ollie whispered. He dialed the number for the hotel but the phone didn't ring. A message popped up on the screen.

"It says there's no service here. I can't even get a signal," Ollie sighed.

"I'm just so worried about Mika's cubs, I can't handle it," Lucy whimpered. She laid her head in Lottie's lap.

"Lucy, you have to stop crying," Ollie said. "Harley is going to hear you."

Lucy lifted her head. "I'm not crying, Ollie, I'm just upset," she said.

But as she looked at him, she could hear crying, too.

"You know what that sounds like?" Lucy said.

"Some really awful violin music screeching?" Lottie guessed.

"No, kittens! It sounds like baby cheetah

cubs crying for their mama. Listen!" Lucy gasped.

The kids listened in silence as the cubs' cries grew louder.

"I think the sound is coming from inside the walls," Ollie said as he pressed his ear to the wall.

"No, the floor. It's coming from the floor," Lucy said as she put her cheek on the wood floor beneath them.

"But how did they crawl under the wood floor? They're not that small," Lottie said.

"There must be a basement," Ollie whispered. Ollie's eyes scanned the closet. "If only we could find a way down there," he said to himself.

Lucy began to pat the walls. "Maybe there's a trap door or something," she said.

"Or even better, a laundry chute," Ollie smiled.

He pointed behind a wall of fluffy folded

towels to a little box on the wall. It had a silver handle with small words written underneath it that said: Soiled Linens.

Lucy pulled the lever and looked down the long, dark laundry chute leading to the basement.

"This must be where Max puts all the dirty towels from the spa," she said.

"Yea, it's much easier than carrying them downstairs to be washed. Our Nana's house has one of those, remember?" Lucy said.

"I remember," Lottie said. "You guys tried to make me slide down it when I was three years old," she said.

"Dad caught us just in time. Still, it would have been fun," Lucy smiled.

"Are you thinking what I'm thinking?" Lottie said with a twinkle in her eye.

"It's really our only way out of here, unless we want to get caught by Harley," Ollie shrugged.

"Ladies first," Ollie said as he peered down the long dark tunnel leading to the basement.

"I'm so nervous," Lucy said. Her teeth chattered as she spoke.

"It's no big deal. Just think of it like a slide," Lottie said. "I need a boost."

Ollie lifted Lottie's leg up and she slid down the laundry chute face-first.

"Wheeeee!" she squealed.

"Shhhh!" Ollie and Lucy both whispered after her.

There was a thud, followed by a long silence.

"Oh no, what if she didn't make it?" Lucy asked as she peered down into the darkness.

It was pitch black at the bottom of the laundry chute, and nobody could see anything.

"Lottie, are you okay?" Ollie called to her.

"Better than okay! That was amazing!" Lottie smiled.

"Then why were you so quiet?" Ollie whispered.

"Because you guys said Shhhh!" Lottie giggled.

Ollie and Lucy looked at each other.

"You're next," Ollie said.

Lucy slid down the slide. She hit a big pile of wet towels the bottom.

A few seconds later, Ollie crashed on the floor behind her. Instead of hearing the cubs meowing, he heard them purring. It sounded like a motor humming in the darkness. Ollie looked over and saw Lucy with the cubs already curled up in her lap.

"I can hardly see anything," Ollie said.

Lucy switched on Harley's phone and shone the flashlight across the room. It was worse than any of them expected.

They were inside a huge stone room with no windows. The only door to the room was locked!

CHAPTER EIGHT

"What is this place? It looks more like a dungeon than a laundry room," Ollie gulped. The room was so dark he could hardly see, except for the cell phone light that Lucy held up.

"Guys, this phone is about to run out of batteries," Lucy said. "We don't have much light. I think we're stuck down here until someone comes to find us."

"You mean, until Harley discovers us," Lottie said. "She'll have to feed the cubs sometime soon. They sound hungry."

"I wonder what she'll do when she finds us," Lottie said.

She could feel a pit growing in her stomach, or maybe that was just the soggy cucumbers she'd eaten earlier.

"There's got to be a way out of here," Ollie said. He pushed against the door but it wouldn't budge. "It figures it would be locked from the inside, too."

"I overheard Garth saying that the maids only work in the morning. They've all gone home for the night, so no one will be down to do laundry until tomorrow," Lucy sighed.

"You mean we could be stuck down here all night?" Lottie said. "This place gives me the creeps."

"Me, too," Ollie shivered.

It was so quiet and spooky in the basement, the only thing they could hear were the cubs purring.

"Lucy, where are you?" Ollie said in the darkness.

"I'm right here," she said as she flipped the phone's flashlight back on. Lucy was covered in three tiny cheetah cubs, who were snuggling against her body for warmth.

"They make a really warm blanket," Lucy giggled.

"Let me see that phone," Ollie said as he shone the phone's flashlight around the corners of the room. White towels and sheets were piled up to the ceiling.

"What's that up there?" Ollie climbed up the mountain of towels all the way to the ceiling. At the top of the pile of towels was a small vent leading outside.

"That looks like a vent for the air to escape," Lottie said. "You know, so it doesn't get too hot in here when they're doing laundry."

"Do you think one of you could squeeze

through the vent?" Ollie said.

"Why us?" Lucy asked. "You're already up there."

"Because I'm the biggest one, I'll never fit," Ollie said.

"I'll go," Lottie said. "Lucy looks too cozy with the cubs to tear her away from them."

Two of the cubs snuggled in Lucy's lap. The third cub was fast asleep around her neck.

Ollie smiled. "That's great, Lottie. I'll help you through the vent. When you're on the other side, go find Garth. But, make sure Harley doesn't see you first."

Ollie boosted Lottie through the small vent. Her head pushed through the opening but she got stuck right at her shoulders.

"It's too small. Or, I'm too big," Lottie whimpered.

"You're going to have to squeeze," Ollie told her as he pushed against her feet.

Lottie wiggled as hard as she could. After a

minute of pushing, she fell onto the ground on the other side of the tiny vent. She scooted out onto the sidewalk, and brushed the dirt off her knees.

As soon as Lottie hopped to her feet, she saw Harley walking around the corner. Harley wore her sunglasses on top of her head and her leopard print purse was flung over her shoulder. Her heels clicked on the sidewalk as she walked towards where Lottie had fallen.

"Run, Lottie! Hurry, before Harley sees you!" Ollie whispered. "We haven't got much time left before sundown."

CHAPTER NINE

Lottie sped around the corner, out of Harley's sight. She bumped straight into Garth, the owner of Safari Park.

"Lucy, or is it Lottie?" he said. "You startled me!"

"Oh, I'm so glad I found you," Lottie said. "You've got to come with me right now. It's the cubs, we've found them."

"The cubs?" Garth gasped. "How did you ever find them?"

"I'll explain on the way," Lottie said. "In the meantime, you've got to call the police."

"The police, why?"

Lottie spotted Harley walking towards them and grabbed Garth by the arm.

"Here, duck down behind this bush," she said. They crouched in a patch of bushes, where Harley couldn't see them as she strolled down the sidewalk.

"It's Harley Hanson," Lottie whispered. "She stole the cubs. We have her phone and all the proof is on it."

"Are you sure?" Garth sputtered.

"One hundred percent sure." Lottie nodded.

"Oh good gracious," Garth gasped. "I'll notify the police. But first, let's go see the cubs."

Lottie led Garth down into the basement of the hotel. Garth took out his key ring and unlocked the heavy door. As soon as the door popped open, the lights came on overhead.

Lucy and Ollie were laying on top of a

mountain of towels, with the three cheetah cubs asleep on their laps.

"Oh my goodness, Mika's babies," Garth shouted. He picked the cubs up and they licked him on his arms.

"Imagine how happy Mika will be to have her cubs back," Lucy smiled.

The kids carried the cheetah cubs upstairs to the hotel lobby while Garth called the police on the front desk phone. He hung up the phone and a serious expression crossed his face.

"They're sending a team of police over to arrest Harley Hanson right now. They'll be here any minute," Garth said.

"I'm so glad," Lucy sighed. "That's one more mystery solved by the LOL Detective club. Case closed."

"In the meantime, let's find Artie and see if he can take the cubs over to Mika," Garth said.

Within a few minutes, a police jeep drove through Safari Park's front gate. Two police officers jumped out and marched into the building.

"Hello, I'm Officer Mikels," the tall police officer said. "We're here to arrest the kidnapper. Any idea where she went?"

"The last I saw her, she was headed towards the restaurant," Lottie said.

The two police officers split up and searched the hotel and the grounds. A few minutes later, they ran back to the hotel lobby.

"Harley Hanson's gone. She's nowhere to be found," Officer Mikels panted.

CHAPTER TEN

"I bet she went down to the basement to check on the cubs and noticed they were gone," Lottie said.

Garth paced the floor. "All the jeeps are still here, so she must have run away on foot."

"Did you see those heels she was wearing? She can't have gone very far," Lucy said. "She's got to be hiding here in the hotel somewhere."

Just then Ollie's face lit up as if he remembered something.

"Guys, do you think she still has her purse with her?"

"Yea, I bet she does. She always kept that thing right next to her," Lucy said.

"Well, remember how when we were in the spa, my tablet accidentally fell into her purse? By the time I figured out my tablet was missing, we were already locked in the closet," Ollie explained.

"I still don't understand, Ollie," Lucy frowned.

"Do you remember last summer when I left my tablet over at my friend Ben's house on accident?" asked Ollie.

"Oh yea, Ben's dog ran off with it, and we found it in his dog house," Lucy giggled.

"Right. Well, remember how we activated that GPS location device and we found it in minutes?" said Ollie.

"I remember that. It was called Find My Tablet, or something," Lottie said.

"If Ollie's tablet is still in Harley's purse, then we can find it in minutes," Lucy squealed.

"Yup, I knew my computer gadgets would come in handy," Ollie beamed.

Garth fired up the hotel's computer and searched for Ollie's username on the Wi-Fi.

"Here we go," he said, as the police looked over his shoulder. Within seconds, a light popped up on the screen showing Harley Hanson's exact location.

"She's up on the roof," Garth yelled.

"Hiding out, no doubt," Lucy said.

The police ran straight up four flights of stairs, all the way up to the rooftop patio. When they flung open the doors, they found Harley Hanson crouched in a corner eating a chocolate bar.

"Arrest this woman at once," Garth shouted. The police handcuffed Harley Hanson and whisked her away to the police station.

"I wonder why she would steal the cubs?"

Ollie wondered.

"Oh, I know exactly why," Garth nodded. "The six million dollars that Harley's grandfather gave us was all the money left in his estate. Harley's pretending to be rich, but she's really broke. I bet she thought that she could fool us into giving her back the money."

"Oh, now I feel bad for her," Lucy sighed.

"Well, there's always a job for her here at the hotel if she wants one," Garth smiled. "In fact, I think I need to hire someone to wash those dirty towels down in the basement. I had no idea the piles were so big," he smiled.

"Harley Hanson doing laundry? Now that's something I'd love to see," Ollie smiled.

The End

Thank you for reading *Cubnapping In Kenya: LOL Detective Club, Book Three.*

If you enjoyed this book, please leave a review on Amazon! I love hearing what my readers think!

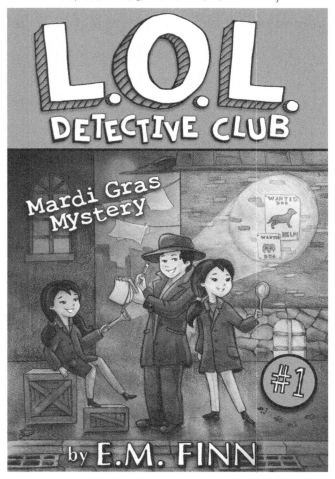

THE PARIS PUZZLER:
LOL DETECTIVE CLUB BOOK #2

And more coming soon!

About The Author

E.M. Finn writes children's books, including The LOL Detective Club Mystery Series.

She lives in Los Angeles with her husband, four daughters, and a Goldendoodle named Daisy.

When she's not writing, she homeschools her children and encourages her husband in his film and television career.

Some of her favorite books include the *Harry Potter* series, *Nancy Drew Mysteries*, *The Boxcar Children*, and the *Little House on the Prairie* books.

Made in the USA
Coppell, TX
19 October 2020